Contents

onlight
Riders

...CIP catalogue record for this book
...vailable from the British Library.

ISBN 978 1 40837 150 3

...in Great Britain by Clays Ltd, Elcograf S.p...

...this book are made from wood from respo...

MIX
Paper from
responsible sources
FSC® C104740
FSC
www.fsc.org

Orchard Books
An imprint of
Hachette Children's Group
Hodder & Stoughton Limited
Carmelite House
Victoria Embankment
London EC4Y 0DZ

Hachette UK Company
www.hachette.co.uk
w.hachettechildrens.co.uk

ORCHARD BOOKS

First published in Great Britain in 2023 by Hodder & Stoughton Limited

1 3 5 7 9 10 8 6 4 2

Text copyright © Hodder & Stoughton Limited 2023
Illustrations copyright © Hodder & Stoughton Limited 2023
The moral rights of the author and illustrator have been asserted.

All characters and events in this publication, other than those clearly in the public domain,
any resemblance to real persons, living or dead, is purely coincidental.

A
is

Printed and bound

The paper and board used in

P
Part o

An

www.

CHAPTER ONE

Amara could feel excitement quiver through Ember as they watched Imogen and her pony, Tide, completing the mug race in their training session. Leaning out of the saddle, Imogen effortlessly grabbed the metal mug that was upside down on top of a pole in the ground, and without Tide slowing she placed it on top of the next pole before galloping over the finish line.

Alex whooped and set off on his stocky

chestnut pony, Rose, riding even faster than Imogen. Grabbing the mugs, he banged them down on the empty poles one after the other without a second's hesitation. Amara longed to be as good as Alex and Imogen, who were both so fast and accurate. They had been in the Moonlight Stables mounted games team for three years now.

Ember fidgeted impatiently as Bea, the youngest team member by two years, set off at a slow, steady canter on Sandy, a pretty palomino pony. Amara patted Ember soothingly. Setting off before the rider in front of her had finished would mean elimination in a competition and Jill, their trainer, was very strict about it, particularly now that the most important competition of the year was coming up in a few days' time –

the mounted games championships.

Steady, Ember, she thought.

I want it to be our turn! Ember replied.

I know, but we have to wait.

Although he looked like an ordinary – if very beautiful – coal-black pony, Ember was an elemental horse, just like all the other ponies in the Moonlight Stables games team. His magic allowed him and Amara to talk to each other with their minds.

There were elemental horses all over the world and each had a power linked to one of the four elements – earth, air, fire and water. Every elemental horse found a True Rider to bond with, someone who could help harness their power and control their magic. Most of the time the horses hid their magic from the world, only transforming into their true elemental form when they needed to practise their magic or help someone in need. The only people who knew about elemental horses were True Riders or Legacy Riders – someone whose parent or grandparent had been a True Rider. They kept the elemental horses' secret safe.

Ember had chosen Amara to be his True Rider very soon after meeting her. She was so glad he had! Not only did she get to do amazing magic with him, but she had lots of non-magical fun with her friends on the mounted games team and their elemental horses. Together they hacked out in the woods, helped at the stables and took part in mounted games competitions, and in the summer they'd all gone to pony camp.

It's our turn! said Ember as Bea and Sandy

finished. He leapt eagerly towards the poles.
Amara's long brown plaits flew out behind
her as her hand closed on the first mug.
Pulling it off the pole, she placed it on the
next pole along. *One down!*

Ears pricked, Ember lengthened his stride
like a racehorse – but now he was going too
fast. Amara grabbed for the next mug but
missed. "Whoa!" she gasped. "Ember, stop!"

Ember spun round and cantered back to the pole so Amara could get the mug. She placed it on to the final pole and they raced over the finish line in good time, but Amara was cross with herself. "I can't believe I messed that up!" she groaned as Ember halted beside Tide.

"Don't worry, everyone makes mistakes and you corrected it quickly," said Imogen. She was the team captain and was always very encouraging.

"At least you were trying to go fast," said Alex, "not like Kalini." He looked at Amara's best friend, Kalini, who'd just set off. She was stopping Thunder beside each pole, very carefully picking up the mug before trotting slowly to the next pole. "You can go faster than that, Kalini!" Alex shouted impatiently.

"Alex, ssh!" said Imogen.

"But we'll never win the championships if she goes that slowly!"

"We won't win if you make her go faster and she misses every mug," Imogen said as Kalini crossed the line. "Good job, Kalini!"

"Yes, well done!" said Amara, knowing Kalini sometimes worried she wasn't good enough to be on the team. "You put both mugs on perfectly. Not like me."

"I was really slow though," said Kalini, pulling a face.

"You'll get faster," Imogen reassured her. She pushed her glasses up her nose. "Now let's practise handovers until Jill gets back." Jill had gone down to the yard to talk to a new client who wanted to book some riding lessons. As well as training the mounted games team and giving the elemental horses a home, Jill ran a riding school with eight non-magical ponies. All the members of the games team helped her out at the weekends and in the holidays.

Now the five of them took it in turns to canter up the school and back again, before handing over a baton to the next rider. Alex, Imogen and Bea had no problem at all, but Ember kept jumping forward before Amara had a proper hold of the baton, making her drop it. Kalini's nerves also kept getting the better of her and she fumbled the baton every time. Alex quickly grew impatient. "Get with it, you two! You can do better than this!"

Amara saw that Kalini was close to tears. "Alex, yelling at us isn't going to help."

"Well, what is?" Alex said hotly. "Because

if you carry on like this, we're going to come last at the championships."

"Alex, stop shouting!" Imogen exclaimed.

"Whoa, what's going on here?" Amara looked round and saw two older riders, Jasmine and Ollie, riding up to the gate on their ponies, Cloud and Sirocco. Jasmine and Ollie had been on the team until recently. They were in their fifth year of secondary school and had to focus on their exams so had given their places up to Amara and Kalini. "We could hear you from the yard," Jasmine went on.

"Alex is being really annoying," said Amara. "He keeps yelling at us and—"

"Because Amara and Kalini's handovers are rubbish!" Alex interrupted loudly.

"Cool it, both of you," said Jasmine. "If Jill

catches you shouting at each other, she'll be furious."

They both simmered down. Jasmine was right. Jill wouldn't tolerate arguing in the team.

"OK, so you want to improve your handovers?" Jasmine said to Amara and Kalini, who nodded. "Well, you need to trust your ponies and you need to make eye contact with the rider you're handing over to."

Ollie nodded. "Your ponies have been trained to gallop until they're over the finish line, so try not to worry where they're going – look at the person you're doing the handover with. If you focus on their face, you'll be able to judge when to take and release the baton."

"We found combining magic together

outside of games practice helped us learn to be in sync," said Jasmine.

"What do you mean?" asked Kalini, puzzled.

Jasmine raised an eyebrow at Ollie. "Should we show them?"

"Sure. Snow?" he said.

Jasmine nodded. They seemed to be able to read each other's thoughts almost as easily as an elemental horse and their True Rider.

Jasmine touched Cloud's neck. Cloud stamped a front hoof on the ground and a small cloud formed above her as she channelled her water magic. Rain started to fall, and Ollie's dark chestnut pony, Sirocco, stamped one of his hooves. A freezing wind swirled past them and wrapped around the cloud. The cold air froze the rain, turning the

droplets to snow. Flakes began to float down.

"Oh, wow!" breathed Amara.

"Ah, combining your magic. Great idea, you two!" Amara saw Jill walking back to the school. She looked at the five younger riders. "Uniting your horses' powers is a really good way to practise working as a team. Maybe the rest of you should try it some time."

"What about me?" asked Bea. "I'm not a True Rider yet, so I can't do that."

"I'm afraid you'll just have to keep practising in a non-magical way for now," said Jill.

Bea looked upset. "I've been riding Sandy for ages. Why hasn't she chosen me?"

"Ponies choose when they're ready," said Jill. "These things can't be rushed."

"It took Sirocco more than a year to ask me," Ollie put in.

"It will happen, Bea," said Jasmine. "I'm sure of it."

Jill looked at the younger girl's downcast face. "Tell you what, how about I teach you some groundwork exercises you can do with

17

Sandy? They're an excellent way of helping a pony and rider bond and build up trust. We can set up a course in the meadow and you can use it whenever you want."

"OK," said Bea, looking more hopeful.

"We've got some time now; we could help you set it up," said Ollie, looking at Jasmine, who nodded.

"Great – thanks," said Jill, opening the gate. "The rest of you can go for a ride in the woods to cool the ponies off. They've worked hard, so go and have some fun."

As they rode out of the school, an exciting thought popped into Amara's head. When they were out in the woods maybe they could try uniting their horses' powers. Jill had said to have fun – well, what could be more fun than doing magic?!

CHAPTER TWO

Leaving Jasmine, Ollie, Bea and Jill carrying poles and equipment down to the meadow where the elemental horses grazed, Amara and the others rode out of the yard. Moonlight Stables was near the end of a narrow, pot-holed lane. Turning to the right from the entrance gate led to the cottages where Amara and her parents lived and the main road that ran through the small town of Eastwall. Turning left led past the

Moonlight Stables paddocks to a wooded hill and an open ridgeway which was perfect for galloping on.

The air was frosty and the ponies' hooves clattered on the stony lane. Although it was still only the middle of the afternoon, the temperature was dropping and Amara was glad she had her winter coat and gloves on. She and Kalini rode side by side.

In front of them, Amara saw Imogen speaking intently to Alex, her usually cheerful face creased into a frown. After a few minutes, Alex's shoulders sagged and he nodded. He reined Rose in and waited for Amara and Kalini to draw alongside them.

"I'm sorry, guys," he said sheepishly. "I shouldn't have had a go at you both."

"That's all right," said Kalini. "Don't worry."

But Amara wasn't prepared to let Alex off the hook that easily. "Shouting at us doesn't help, you know."

"I know," Alex sighed. "And I really am sorry. Friends again?"

Amara nodded. "Sure. Friends again." Alex's ADHD meant he sometimes struggled to control his emotions, especially his temper, and often acted without thinking, but she knew that he genuinely felt bad afterwards and always meant it when he apologised. "But try not to yell at us any more, OK?"

"OK," said Alex. "I'll try." Amara saw Imogen throw him a smile.

"How about to make up for being an idiot, I get us all a hot chocolate and cake at Marco's after we've finished at the yard?" Alex was always generous with his allowance.

"Great!" said Amara. Kalini was staying at hers that night and they had no plans apart from staying in, watching a movie and doing online pony quizzes.

"Suits me," said Imogen. "I'll text Mum and ask her to pick me up a bit later."

Alex grinned as they entered the woods. "So, who wants a race to the big oak tree?"

"We're supposed to be cooling the ponies off," Imogen reminded him.

"We can do that afterwards," he said. "Come on, Immy. It'll be fun."

She gave in. "OK then. On your marks . . . get set . . . GO!"

The ponies thundered along the wide track that led up the hill. Amara felt happiness rush through her as Ember stretched his neck out, his hooves throwing up fallen leaves as they raced beside the other ponies. She loved galloping!

They reached the oak tree together and brought the ponies to a halt, then they rode through the woods, chatting about the competition. Every so often, Amara looked round, thinking she'd heard the sound of a hoof kicking a stone or the clink of a pony's bit as it tossed its head – but no other horses or riders appeared.

"We've got to practise really hard for the next few days," said Alex as the path twisted and turned. "We have to beat Storm Stables."

They all nodded. They always wanted to beat their rivals.

Storm Stables was a smart equestrian centre owned by a horrible woman called

Ivy Thornton. Ivy was a True Rider who had turned bad – a Night Rider. She had four elemental horses on her yard and was always trying to get more so she could use their powers for her evil plans. She and Jill had been friends when they were younger, but when Jill's elemental horse, Shula, had died in an accident, they had become bitter enemies. Amara and the others didn't know exactly what had happened, but afterwards, Jill had devoted her life to providing a safe home for elemental horses and helping them find their True Riders.

The Storm Stables team were in the championships along with the Moonlight Stables team and teams from Hillside Farm Riding School and Long Lane Stables.

"Why don't we do what Jill said and see if

combining our powers helps our teamwork?" said Amara. They were passing a frozen pond, and seeing the ice had given her an idea.

"What are you thinking?" asked Imogen curiously.

Amara pointed at the pond. "If Ember uses his fire magic to melt the ice, Tide could use her water magic to swirl the water into the air, then Thunder could use his air magic to make the water into some kind of shape and Rose . . ." She frowned. Rose had earth magic and she was very good at making plants grow, but Amara couldn't see quite how that would fit in. "Rose could—

"We'll think of something," interrupted Alex eagerly.

"Do you think it's safe to do magic here?"

asked Kalini. "What if someone sees us?"

Amara remembered the noises she'd heard earlier, but the woods were silent now apart from the occasional flurry of birdsong high up in the trees. "There's no one here. I'm sure we'll be fine."

"OK. Let's do it," said Imogen. "Ready, everyone?"

"Ready!" they all cried.

The four ponies reared up and transformed into majestic elemental horses – becoming taller and more muscular. Ember's mane and tail turned into flickering flames and Tide's frothed like sea foam; Rose's became a mossy green decorated with flowers and Thunder's swirled like black clouds. Their eyes sparkled in different colours – Ember's bright amber, Thunder's coal black, Rose's shining silver and Tide's deep blue.

Amara could feel the elemental magic flowing through Ember and into her. It made every centimetre of her skin tingle, and her heart sang.

Ready, Ember? she thought, excitement beating through her.

Ready!

She felt his enthusiasm as he stamped his front hooves down on to the ground. Two balls of fire shot away and landed on the frozen pond. They exploded, flames spreading across the surface, making the ice crack and melt.

Amara glanced at Imogen. Her face was creased in concentration as Tide took over from Ember. Using her powers, she swept the icy water upwards into a cloud and then it was Thunder's turn. He reared up and stamped his hooves down. A blast of icy air instantly hit the cloud and it started to fall as snow. Thunder stamped his hooves again and the air currents obeyed him, turning the snow into the shape of a Christmas tree.

The others laughed in delight.

"Awesome, Thunder!" exclaimed Amara, delight exploding through her. Doing magic with her friends and their horses was the best feeling ever!

"Our turn now!" shouted Alex.

The next moment, Rose banged her hooves down, making white water lilies appear all over the Christmas tree's branches.

Imogen and Amara clapped.

The tree suddenly started to wobble from side to side. "Whoa, Thunder's losing control of the magic!" cried Kalini. "Be careful, Thun—"

She broke off with a shriek as the Christmas tree exploded and icy rain and water lily petals rained down on top of them. Everyone squealed and the horses shook their manes, transforming back into their pony forms in their surprise.

"We're soaked!" exclaimed Amara, looking at her sodden jodhpurs and Ember's dripping mane. The other horses and their riders were just as wet.

Thunder looked at them sheepishly from under his thick forelock.

"Sorry!" Kalini giggled. "He said he just couldn't control the power any longer."

Alex chuckled. "Well, Jill did tell us to cool the ponies off."

"She didn't mean for us to freeze to death though!" said Imogen.

I'll help dry everyone, Ember thought eagerly. He stamped his hooves, setting fire to a fallen log beside the pond.

They all gathered round it, the flames warming them up before Tide put the fire out by drawing up some of the water from the pond and splashing it over the remains of the log.

"A canter along the ridgeway should help us finish drying off," said Alex.

"And then we'd better get back," said Imogen, looking up at the sky. Although it was only mid-afternoon, the winter sun was already starting to sink towards the horizon. "We don't want to be out when it gets dark."

They cantered up the hill through the trees. At the highest point, the woods opened out on to an area of clear high ground covered with short grass – the ridgeway. There were steep drops on either side and on a clear day it was possible to see all of Eastwall, but now the buildings were shrouded in mist.

The ponies went on, their hooves sending pebbles skittering away as they leapt over rabbit holes and rocks. After a canter, they slowed to a trot then turned for home, but as they approached the trees, a dense grey fog started rolling across the top of the ridgeway like smoke, hiding the entrance to the bridleway that led down to the stables.

Ember and the other horses whickered in alarm.

"Whoa, that fog appeared quickly," said Imogen. "We'd better get home."

Urging the ponies on, they rode into the billowing fog. It closed around them, the freezing cold taking their breath away.

"I can't see anything!" said Amara, peering anxiously through the grey, alarm prickling through her.

"Me neither," said Alex, close by.

"I can't see where the bridlepath is," said Kalini. "Which way do we go?"

Amara's stomach twisted into knots. Like Kalini, she was losing her sense of direction. What if one of them rode the wrong way and ended up falling down the steep slope?

"Phone torches!" said Alex, pulling out his phone. He tried to use the torch app but its thin beam of light was instantly swallowed up.

Amara heard Thunder stumble and Kalini gasp. "Are you OK?" Amara asked anxiously.

"Yes," Kalini said shakily. "But Thunder can't see where his hooves are going."

Neither can I, Ember told Amara. Sensing the anxiety pulsing through the pony, she put a hand on his neck to calm him.

"OK, stop, everyone," said Imogen. "Someone's going to get injured if we keep going. We need to think how we can get safely to the bridlepath."

Amara swallowed and looked round at the swirling fog. Imogen was right, but it seemed impossible. There were steep drops on either side and rabbit holes in the ground that could cause the ponies to stumble and hurt themselves. Fear gripped her. What were they going to do?

CHAPTER THREE

"Standing still's not going to help us, Immy," said Alex impatiently. "The entrance to the bridleway can't be far. Follow me, everyone!"

"No, Alex, wait!" said Imogen.

"Let's get off and lead the ponies so we can check the ground is safe for them," said Kalini. "If we tread in a rabbit hole, we'll just trip, but if they do, they might break a leg."

"Kalini's right," said Amara, starting to dismount. The last thing she wanted was for

Ember to hurt himself.

But Alex didn't listen. Through the fog, Amara made out a shadowy shape moving as he urged Rose on. "I'm sure it's this way, guys. Come on before we freeze to . . ." Alex broke off with a yell as Rose fell to her knees. He flew over her shoulders with a loud thump as he hit the frozen ground.

"Alex? Rose? Are you OK?" Amara left Ember and made her way towards them, her hands groping in the fog where she had seen Alex fall. To her right, she could hear Rose scrambling to her feet. Reaching down, Amara's hands found Alex's back.

"I'm just winded . . ." Alex said, fighting to get his breath back. "Not hurt . . . I'll be fine . . . in a minute."

Taking Amara's hand, Alex got to his

feet. He stumbled over to Rose and put his arms round her neck. "Rose, are you really all right? I'm sorry." There was a moment's silence as they spoke with their thoughts, then Alex sighed in relief. "Rose is OK," he told the others. "She says she's grazed her knees but that's all." He shivered. "What are we going to do? We can't stay out here all night. We'll die of cold."

"Amara, Ember might be able to help," said Kalini suddenly. "Fog is made of tiny droplets of water. If Ember uses his magic to make a big fireball, it might burn away the fog."

I'll try! Ember said to Amara.

Amara quickly mounted and Ember transformed. In the light from his flaming mane and tail she could see her friends' worried faces.

Come on, Ember! she thought, hoping Kalini's idea would work.

Ember stamped his hooves and a huge fireball appeared. Amara could feel the power he was using to stop it shooting away into the distance. The fog around it vanished as the flames warmed the air.

"The fireball is burning some of the fog

away. But only the fog closest to it!" she said.

I think we can still use it to help us find the path, Ember said.

Concentrating hard, he used his mind to roll the fireball slowly forward. Its heat burned away the fog, leaving a clear path behind it. Ember walked after it and the other ponies and riders followed.

After a little while, Amara saw the yellow wooden post that marked the entrance to the bridlepath in the trees. "We're going the right way!"

As they reached the treeline, Ember stopped. He was panting. Amara could tell that creating and controlling such a huge fireball was using a lot of energy.

I can't take it any further, he told Amara. *It would be too dangerous in the trees. They'll catch fire if I get too close.*

We should be fine from here, Amara said. *We can follow the path down.*

Ember let the fireball splutter out and transformed back to his pony form. Amara rode on to the bridlepath and felt a rush of relief. The fog was much thinner in the trees, fading to a fine mist and then clearing completely as they got further down the hill.

"That was really scary," said Kalini as they finally rode out on to the lane. "We could have been lost up there for ages. I didn't know fog could appear so suddenly. One minute it wasn't there, the next it was."

"I know," said Imogen. "I've never been caught out like that before. Thank you, Ember."

Kalini and Alex echoed her thanks.

Ember snorted. Amara could tell that although he was tired, he was very happy that he'd been able to help.

They rode on towards the stables, passing the meadow which now had a collection of poles, cones and other equipment laid out in a course. "That must be where they were doing the groundwork," said Imogen. "I wonder how Bea and Sandy got on."

"I hope it helps Sandy choose Bea to be her True Rider," said Kalini. "If I were Bea, I'd hate to be the only one on the team who isn't a True Rider yet."

Amara agreed. She could completely understand Bea's longing to be able to be part of the magical world.

Do you think Sandy will ask Bea to be her True Rider one day? she asked Ember as they turned up the driveway.

I'm sure she will, he said. *She isn't the kind of pony who rushes into things; she's calm and patient. I think she doesn't feel Bea is quite ready to be a True Rider yet and that's why she's waiting.*

Amara leant down and hugged his neck. *I'm very glad you didn't wait.*

Ember turned his head to nuzzle her. *I knew the moment I saw you that you were right for me,* he said. *I couldn't have waited even a day longer.* Amara's heart swelled with happiness and she felt a warm glow from her head to her toes.

Back on the yard, they brushed the ponies down and gave them thick straw beds to lie down in and bulging nets of hay to eat before taking the saddles to the tack room.

It was a wooden building that doubled as the office where Jill checked riders in for their lessons. There was a heater, a kitchen area, some comfy chairs and a desk as well as rows of saddle holders attached to the walls with bridle hooks underneath, chests where the grooming kits were kept and shelves of riding helmets and body protectors. It smelled of saddle soap and leather and was one of Amara's favourite places. Ollie and Jasmine had left, but Bea was cleaning a bridle as she waited for her dad to pick her up.

"How was your groundwork session with Sandy?" Kalini asked as they put their tack and helmets away.

Bea smiled. "It was good. I led her in, out and over grids of poles, over a mini seesaw and across some tarpaulin on  the floor, guiding her mainly with my voice and a long thin stick which I had to use to point where I wanted her to go. Sandy had a headcollar and leadrope on but Jill said when we have built up the trust between us, she won't need them. I'll be able to guide her just with gestures and voice commands."

"That sounds cool," said Imogen.

"It is, but . . ." A look of frustration crossed Bea's face. "I really wish Sandy would choose me to be her True Rider so we could do magic with the rest of you."

"I'm sure it'll happen one day," Amara reassured her, remembering what Ember had said.

"But what if it doesn't?" said Bea gloomily. "What if I'm just not the right rider for Sandy and she never chooses me? Maybe I should be looking at one of the other ponies who hasn't got a True Rider yet, like Forest. He's sweet."

"Forest?" Amara asked. Forest was a young dark bay elemental horse who had only started being ridden that year. He was nervous and flighty.

"I don't think Forest would be right for you," said Imogen. "Jill told me she's not sure he'll ever be a competitive games pony – he finds competitions too stressful."

"But if he was with his True Rider, he might be more confident," said Bea.

"Maybe," said Imogen doubtfully.

Bea's phone pinged. She checked it. "That's my dad. See you all tomorrow," she said, putting the bridle she'd been cleaning away on its peg.

"Yep, see you, Bea," everyone chorused.

As Bea left, they all looked at each other. "I really don't think Forest would be the right elemental horse for her," said Imogen.

"I know. Sandy's perfect – they make such a good pair," said Kalini.

Amara nodded. "I hope Sandy chooses her soon."

CHAPTER FOUR

It was a twenty-minute walk to Marco's Ice Cream Parlour on the High Street. By the time they got there, their cheeks were pink from the cold. Marco's had tables in the centre and booths along one wall, the seats covered in red leather. They ordered mugs of hot chocolate and slices of cake – red velvet for Imogen and Amara, chocolate fudge for Alex and carrot cake with frosting for Kalini.

As they were waiting for their order to

arrive, a girl about their age came in with her mum.

"Let's get a cake to take home to cheer you up," the girl's mum was saying.

Imogen nudged Alex. "Isn't that Amy from the Hillside Farm team? She's in your maths group at school, isn't she?"

He put down the cardboard drinks coaster he was fidgeting with. "Yeah, you're right. Hey, Amy!" he called as the woman behind the counter started to box up the cake Amy had just chosen.

Amy looked round. "Oh, hi," she said, leaving her mum and coming over.

"How's your team's training going?" said Alex. "I warn you, we are doing awesome!"

To Amara's surprise, Amy didn't grin at Alex's teasing. "It's good your training's going

well," she sighed. "Ours was going well ... until today."

"What do you mean?" said Alex, dropping his teasing tone as he heard the unhappiness in her voice.

"Spot – Josh's pony – injured himself this morning when we were out for a ride."

"Oh no, that's awful," said Amara. The others all nodded. Although they really wanted to win the championships, none of them would ever wish for a pony to get injured.

"The vet thinks he'll be OK in a few

weeks," said Amy, "But it means we're down to four riders for the competition, and if anything happens to one of the other ponies we'll have to withdraw."

Mounted games teams needed at least four riders in a team in order to compete, but they usually had five so that one pony and rider could rest during each race. Having five riders also meant that they could pick the four pony and rider pairs who were best for each race. Only having four riders was a definite disadvantage.

"I'm really sorry," said Imogen.

"How did he hurt himself?" asked Alex.

"We were out hacking near our stables and got caught in fog," said Amy.

Amara felt shock run through her. "Fog?"

Amy nodded. "It came out of nowhere and

Spot stepped in a rabbit hole."

"That's terrible," said Kalini, swapping alarmed looks with the others.

Amy's mum called to her. "Are you coming, Ames?"

"Sure. I'll see you all at the finals on Saturday – if we don't have any more injuries," said Amy, crossing her fingers.

They said goodbye and as the door shut behind her, they stared at each other.

"A thick fog that came out of nowhere?" said Imogen. "Exactly the same thing that happened to us."

"And on the same day," added Kalini, "That can't be a coincidence."

"And we all know who can conjure fog," said Alex grimly. "Haze." Haze was one of the Storm Stables elemental horses. "Although

I've never known her make a fog as thick as the one we got caught in today."

Amara remembered the noises she'd heard in the woods – the hoofbeats, the jingle of a bit. "Maybe Haze and the others were in the woods when we were there. Do you think they'd do something like that?"

"They're definitely mean enough," said Kalini.

"And Ivy really wants to win the championships," said Alex. "Storm Stables is in the running to win Yard of the Year for the Central region."

"What's that?" said Amara, who had only moved to Eastwall that spring.

"It's a league table for yards in our region who have riders competing at big events," Imogen explained. "Every win a rider gets, no matter what the discipline, earns their yard points. The bigger the competition, the more points they get. Storm Stables is doing really well. Winning the mounted games final would secure their place at the top of the league."

"So Ivy could be trying to sabotage the other teams," said Amara.

"Do you think anything's happened to the Long Lane team yet?" said Kalini.

"We need to find out," said Imogen.

Amara frowned. "But how?"

The answer came that evening. Amara heard her dad telling her mum he had to go over to Long Weston village the next morning to collect some fence posts. Long Weston was where Long Lane Stables was.

"Can Kalini and I come with you?" said Amara.

"Of course," said her dad. "But why?"

"We'd like to just call at Long Lane Stables and wish the team there luck," said Amara.

Her mum smiled. "Very sportsmanlike of you."

"Well, sure. It's no problem to take you, and I can run you back here afterwards. Be ready to leave at nine," said her dad.

"We will," said Amara.

She and Kalini left the kitchen. "That was lucky," whispered Amara. "Now we can find out if the Long Lane team have been caught in fog too."

"Or if anything else strange has happened to them," said Kalini. She bit her lip anxiously. "Do you think the Storm Stables riders really are trying to cause trouble, Amara?"

Amara's stomach twisted. She wouldn't put anything past Ivy and her three Storm Stables riders!

CHAPTER FIVE

Amara's dad dropped them off the next
morning. "Call me when you've finished and
I'll pick you up."

"Thanks," said Amara. She could see
the Long Lane team in a field on the other
side of the hedge they were next to. There
were five riders warming up for a training
session. Two of them were trotting side by
side, holding a rope between them, while
the other three were practising picking up a

plastic bottle from the top of a barrel.

Amara and Kalini went to the gate. A bridleway sign pointed up one edge of the field, leading into some woods at the far end.

"Hi!" Amara called, waving.

The two riders with the rope – Lily and Casey – recognised them and cantered over.

Casey grinned. "Hi. What are you doing here? Come to spy on us?" she teased.

"Only a little bit," said Amara with a smile. "My dad was coming over this way so we thought we'd come with him and wish you luck. How's your training going?"

"Pretty well," said Lily. "We're practising every day now school's broken up."

"No one's been injured?" said Kalini.

Lily looked surprised. "No."

"How about you?" Casey asked. "How's

your training going?"

"Good," said Amara. She frowned, her eyes catching a movement in the woods at the end of the field. Were there some horses and riders over there? She saw a faint flash of blue in the trees and then felt a tremble run through the ground beneath her feet.

Lily and Casey's ponies both jumped in surprise.

"Whoa! What was that?" Casey said.

Amara started to climb the gate, her eyes fixed on the trees. There was another flash of blue and she caught a glimpse of a stocky bay horse rearing up in the shadows.

The ground started to shake again, harder this time, and then there was a loud tearing, crashing sound. To Amara's horror, an enormous crack opened up in front of the barrel that one of the team members was cantering towards. The black-and-white pony shied violently, throwing his rider off. She hit the ground and the pony turned and raced away, his reins flapping dangerously around his body.

The other four riders struggled to control

their own ponies, who were leaping about in fear.

"Quick!" Amara gasped to Kalini. If the black-and-white pony put his foot through the reins, he would hurt himself. The pony galloped towards the hedge and for a heart-stopping moment, Amara thought he might try to jump it and end up on the road, but to her relief he skidded to a halt. Amara and Kalini sprinted towards him.

"Whoa now, wh-oa!" soothed Kalini, pulling a bag of treats out of her pocket. The pony's eyes flickered towards her.

Kalini and Amara both stopped, knowing running at him would only make him take off again.

Kalini held out a treat. "Come here, boy." Speaking gently, she approached the frightened pony. Amara held her breath as the pony slowly allowed Kalini to take his reins.

Kalini fed him the treat and took him to his rider, who was being helped to her feet. She looked shaken but luckily didn't seem badly injured.

"Are you OK?" Kalini called.

"Yeah, just bruised. Thank you so much!" the pony's rider said, limping over. "I thought Rocky was going to tread on his reins or jump out." She glanced back at the huge crack in the ground. "What just happened?"

"It must have been a mini earthquake or something," said Lily.

Quake. Amara's scalp prickled. One of the Storm Stables elemental horses was called Quake. He had power over the earth and looked just like the horse she had seen rearing in the trees, but she'd never known him to cause so much damage from such a distance away before.

"We'd better move the equipment away from that crack and get back to warming up," Lily said to Amara and Kalini. "Thanks for helping."

"No problem," said Amara. "We'll see you on Saturday."

The five riders set to work, but Rocky refused to go anywhere near the barrel. Every time his rider tried to get him closer, he ran backwards.

"He's really spooked," said Kalini. "Amara, this has to be the work of the Night Riders from Storm Stables."

Amara nodded. "I know, and we can't let

them get away with this. We have to stop the Night Riders before someone gets seriously hurt!"

CHAPTER SIX

"Where have you two been?" said Imogen, who was sweeping the yard outside Tide's stable with Bea when Amara and Kalini arrived. The ponies were tied up and Ember whinnied when he saw Amara.

Alex looked out of Rose's stable. "We've mucked out all these stables, helped Jill with the riding school stables and filled all the water buckets."

"Sorry," said Amara, going over to say hi to

Ember. "We'll make it up to you but wait till you hear what we've just seen."

She and Kalini told them what had happened.

"There was a horse like Quake in the trees," Amara said.

"But we were quite far away. It could have been a different elemental horse," said Kalini. "A more powerful one. We've never seen Quake create a huge crack in the ground like that before."

"Where's Jill?" said Amara. "We need to tell her about this."

"She's teaching," said Imogen. "Let's groom the ponies then speak to her when she's finished."

They fetched the grooming kits. As they returned to the ponies, Amara saw Bea take

a carrot out from her pocket. Sandy's ears
pricked, but to Amara's surprise, Bea walked
right past her and went over to Forest.
Breaking the carrot in two, she fed him half.
Amara saw the confusion on Sandy's face
and felt a prickle of concern. Had Bea been
serious the day before when she'd been
wondering whether she should give up on
Sandy and try a different pony?

Her concern deepened when Bea just gave
Sandy a quick brush over and then moved on
to Forest.

"Why are you grooming Forest, not Sandy,
Bea?" she asked.

Bea's cheeks turned pink. "I just thought I
would. He doesn't get much attention."

"Malia grooms him," Amara pointed out.
Malia was another friend of theirs at the

stables. She competed in high level dressage competitions with her pony, Goldie. She wasn't a True Rider or a Legacy Rider so she didn't know about the elemental horses, but when she hung round with the rest of the gang, Amara had noticed she often fussed over Forest and groomed him.

"Well, she's not here today," said Bea. "And I think he likes me." She stroked Forest's nose. "And I like him."

Sandy pawed the ground unhappily and then jumped back with a surprised snort as a swirling funnel of sand appeared a few metres away from her.

The other ponies whinnied in alarm as the funnel began to spin towards them all. Grains of sand shot off it, grazing their skin.

"Ember! Do something!" Amara cried,

shielding her face with her arm.

I don't know what I can do! Fire can't help!

The ponies panicked, pulling back against the leadropes tying them to the fence.

For a moment, Amara thought the approaching mini sand tornado was going to reach them, but then Thunder banged his hooves down and an enormous gust of wind swept past, whisking Amara's plaits and Ember's mane into the air and sending the grooming kits and water buckets flying. The wind hit the spinning funnel and it exploded. They all shrieked and covered their eyes with their hands, the ponies ducking their heads as the grains of sand rained down around them.

There was a moment's stunned silence.

"Sandy!" said Bea, breaking it. "What did you do that for?"

Sandy hung her head and snorted apologetically.

"It's OK," said Amara, hurrying over to

stroke the palomino pony. "She didn't mean to do it. You know that elemental horses sometimes struggle to control their powers when they haven't got a True Rider."

"Yeah – it's OK, Sandy, don't worry," said Imogen. "Come on, everyone, grab a yard brush. Let's sweep this sand up."

They quickly brushed the sand into a pile and picked up the grooming kits and buckets. Amara glanced at Sandy. She was still looking upset that her power had erupted in such a way. *Oh, Sandy, please just choose Bea,* Amara thought.

They had just finished clearing up the sand when Jill came to find them. "OK, everyone. Time to tack up!"

"Jill, we need to talk to you," said Imogen.

They told her about the fog and the mini

earthquake and their suspicions about Storm Stables. Jill's frown deepened as she listened. "This is very worrying."

"Can we go over to Storm Stables at lunchtime and see if we can find anything out?" Alex asked eagerly.

Jill nodded. "All right, but no going on the yard. You mustn't go on to another yard uninvited."

They all gave vague nods. They did know that rule, but they didn't always stick to it!

"Can I go with them?" asked Bea eagerly.

"Sorry, Bea," said Jill. "It's quite a long ride. If the other horses use their magic to transform, they'll be able to get there and back quickly. You and Sandy wouldn't be able to keep up."

Bea's face fell.

"We'll tell you everything that happens as soon as we get back," Imogen promised.

"And you can do some more groundwork with Sandy while you're waiting," said Jill.

"But I don't want to do groundwork, I want to do magic!" Bea burst out. "It's not fair!" Folding her arms, she walked off looking upset.

"Poor Bea. It's really hard for her not being able to join in," said Kalini sympathetically. "I wish Sandy would choose her."

"I know, but that's out of our control," said Jill, with a sigh. "Sandy will decide when she's ready. Come on, all of you. Time for training!"

CHAPTER SEVEN

The practice didn't go very well. Amara couldn't stop thinking about Storm Stables and she was very distracted, going too fast and unable to stop in time to pick things up. Kalini, Imogen and Alex all seemed to be struggling too. Kalini kept fumbling the handovers, Alex got told off for kicking a mug angrily across the school after he'd mucked up the exercise twice in a row, and even Imogen got cross – which hardly ever happened – and snapped at Tide for fidgeting when she was trying to pile up a tower of plastic cartons. Bea, meanwhile, was still clearly upset after the conversation she'd had with Jill the day before. She burst into tears when she fell over trying to vault on to Sandy.

They were all glad when Jill brought the practice to an end early. "You're going to have to do better than this if you want to do well in the competition," she said, shaking her head. "It's only two days away."

"If we all get there in one piece," muttered Amara to Kalini.

Leaving Bea to do some groundwork with Sandy, they set off for Storm Stables. It was freezing cold and the clouds were heavy and grey above them. In their elemental forms, the horses could gallop far faster than any normal horse could and soon the four of them were speeding along the ridgeway, their manes and tails streaming out behind them.

Amara let all her worries fade away, losing herself in the drumming of Ember's hooves and the feel of the icy wind whipping into her face.

As they got closer to Storm Stables, the horses transformed back into ponies. They stopped at the side of the ridgeway where they could see the stables through a gap in the trees.

Amara and the others dismounted.

It was too risky to leave the horses on their own. Ivy was always looking for more elemental horses to add to her stables and Amara wouldn't put it past her to have something magical that would stop their ponies from escaping if she got her hands on them. She'd once tried to capture Ember using a binding halter that stopped any horse who was wearing it from using their magic and forced them to obey her.

"I'll stay with the horses," offered Kalini. "But don't be too long. Thunder says the air feels like there's snow coming. We don't want to get caught in a blizzard."

"It sounds like there's a training session going on," said Imogen, nodding towards the large indoor arena on the far side of the car park. The double entrance doors were open and they could hear Ivy's voice coming from inside.

"For heaven's sake, get it together, everyone. Stop dithering, Daniela . . . Commit to the pick-up, Shannon. Do I have to tell you the same thing every single time? Get those ponies moving!"

"Come on," said Alex impatiently. Checking that there was no one in the car park, he slipped through the gap in the fence and started to run across the parking area, pausing every now and then behind lorries and trailers. Amara and Imogen followed him.

Outside the entrance to the indoor arena there was a pile of show jumps. Amara, Alex and Imogen crouched among them and peered inside. The air felt icy in the shadows, making Amara shiver, but she soon forgot about the cold as her attention was caught by what was going on inside the arena.

She could see the three elemental horses,

Scorch, Haze and Quake, being ridden by
Zara, Shannon and Daniela. Scorch was
a bright chestnut fire horse; Haze was a
slender, iron-grey water horse with a pure
white mane and tail; and Quake was a stocky
bright bay earth horse with strong legs and
a thick, arched neck. As well as the three
elemental horses, there were two

non-magical games ponies ridden by
Lorenzo and Duncan, two boys who Ivy had
recruited to be part of her mounted games
team. She had built the team around Zara
and Daniela when they had joined Storm
Stables from Moonlight Stables, after Ember
had chosen Amara to be his True Rider
instead of Zara. Amara knew it was the
reason why Zara hated her so much. Zara
had longed to be Ember's True Rider.

All five riders were dressed in long-sleeved
royal blue tops with the Storm Stables logo
embroidered in gold on the back. The ponies
had protective blue boots on their legs,
blue saddlecloths under their saddles and
specialist matching mounted games rope
reins that clipped to their bits.

They were taking it in turns to race up

and down a line of upright poles, weaving
around the poles, turning incredibly swiftly
at the top and thundering back down, each
rider passing a baton to the next rider,
who then set off. Ivy watched, her eyes
narrowed critically. She tapped a riding crop
impatiently against one of her shining black
boots as she shouted:

"Faster, Shannon! Eyes on the baton, Zara!"

Amara watched in awe as the Storm
Stables ponies flew up and down the arena.
They were all so fast, particularly Scorch,
Haze and Quake. She couldn't remember
seeing them gallop so quickly in their pony
form before.

Ivy gave a satisfied nod as they finished.

"Better." She turned to the two stable
hands who were standing at the side of the

school. "Flag race to finish." They hurried to a pile of equipment and set about putting the flags and flag holders out.

Amara glanced at the riders. They looked tired and fed up, as if they'd been practising for hours. The ponies looked cross too. Quake and Haze were shaking their heads and stamping irritably while Scorch was rubbing the side of her face against one of her front legs as if something was irritating her. There was none of the usual chat and laughter of the Moonlight Stables sessions.

When the equipment was ready, Ivy blew her whistle. Moving to the start line, Lorenzo, Duncan and their ponies completed their legs of the race with no mistakes, the boys skilfully placing the flags correctly in all the flag holders. The three girls had less luck. Daniela and Zara missed a handover and Shannon knocked the flag holder over when she put her flag inside.

"That was useless!" snapped Ivy, striding over to them at the end. "You'll do it again and again until you get it right. You will not stop until it's perfect! I expect more of you than this." She pointed with her crop at the flags. "Get practising."

Lorenzo put his hand up as the girls lined up again. "Ivy, do we have to do it again? Sonny's getting tired."

"No, you and Duncan may finish now," said Ivy. "Good job, boys."

Looking relieved, the boys dismounted.

Ivy clicked her fingers at the stable hands, who ran over and took the ponies from them. Duncan and Lorenzo walked off together through the side door. Amara, Imogen and Alex ducked down as the grooms led the ponies out past them.

Ivy made the girls practise the flag race over and over again until they all did it perfectly. She blew her whistle and they stopped near the exit. The ponies were breathing hard and the girls all looked sulky.

"Well, finally, that's good enough," Ivy said. "I don't know why you made such a song and dance about it!"

None of the girls spoke. Scorch rubbed the side of her mouth against one of her front legs again; the other two ponies flattened their ears and tossed their heads. "I hope you understand how important this final is," Ivy went on. "I expect you to do everything in your power to win. Understand?"

The girls nodded. Ivy's eyes raked over them.

"Practising, training, using magic," she continued, ticking the things off on her fingers. "You've done well so far sabotaging the other teams, but you're not working hard enough for the competition itself. You're all clever girls. I am sure you can think of ways to make sure you win." Amara felt a shiver run down her spine as Ivy's voice turned icy hard. "Daniela, use Quake's powers to create a tremor as one of your rivals reaches to pick up a bottle. It will fall over and slow them down. Shannon, a puff of mist just as a pony is racing towards a barrel will make it shy backwards. Zara, the mugs are metal. Heat one up just as one of the other team members picks it up and they'll drop it in shock. You've got control of your ponies' power, so use it."

Amara's thoughts tumbled in confusion. *What does Ivy mean? Riders don't control elemental powers; the horses do.*

There was a metallic clink and suddenly Scorch ran backwards, one rein flapping free from the bit, her dark eyes suddenly flashing with spirit. Amara realised that by rubbing her face she had managed to undo the clip that attached the rein to the metal ring bit in her mouth. Zara yelled in shock, the rapid movement unseating her. Scorch reared up, and Zara slithered inelegantly over her hindquarters and landed on the ground. Amara's hands flew to her mouth in alarm as Scorch's front hooves thudded back down perilously close to Zara's outstretched hands.

Scorch reared up again but in the next moment Ivy was beside her, and in one swift movement she grabbed the dangling blue rope rein and clipped it back on to the bit.

"That. Will. Do!" Ivy snapped, yanking

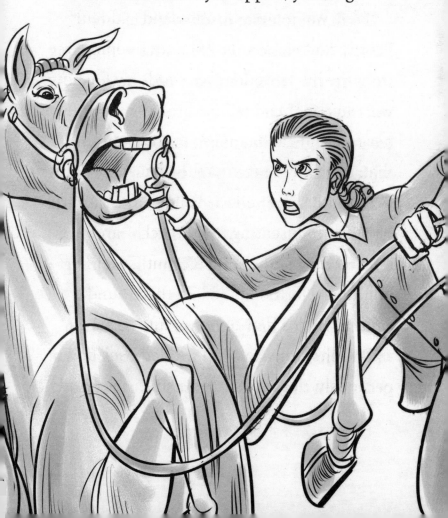

the rein hard with each word. Scorch stopped rearing and stood on all four feet, her eyes flashing furiously. Amara was sure the chestnut horse wanted to fight, but something seemed to be stopping her.

"I will not tolerate disobedience!" Ivy hissed. She glanced at Zara, who was getting up gingerly. "Take her," she said, holding out the rein. "And tell the groom she gets no treats tonight." She pointed at the entrance with her crop. "Take them in."

Zara led Scorch towards the entrance with her two friends following on their ponies. Amara saw Daniela and Shannon exchange concerned looks.

Amara, Alex and Imogen crouched deep in the shadows of the jumps as Zara and the others left the arena. Amara's heart thudded in her chest, hoping Alex would manage to stay still without fidgeting. If Zara, Shannon or Daniela saw them, they would be in serious trouble. A couple of white flakes landed on her arm and she glanced up at the heavy grey sky. Thunder had been right about the snow.

"Are you OK?" she heard Shannon ask Zara in a low voice.

"I'm fine," snapped Zara. "Stupid horse." She glared at Scorch, who glared back.

"The horses don't like these binding reins," said Daniela. "Quake's been trying to get his off too."

"Well, they'll just have to get used to them," said Zara, her voice as hard as Ivy's. "There's no way we're going to let any of the other teams beat us, especially Moonlight Stables.

We'll do whatever it takes to win. OK?"

Shannon nodded, and after some brief hesitation Daniela nodded too.

"Good. Then listen up. I've got an idea of what we can do next . . ."

Zara's voice became too faint to hear as they continued on towards the big barn where the horses were kept. Risking a glance into the arena, Amara saw Ivy stalking out through the side door.

"Oh, wow," breathed Alex, staring at them, his eyes wide. "This is so not good."

"We can't talk about it here," Imogen whispered. "If Ivy finds out what we've just seen, we'll be in serious danger."

Amara nodded, her gaze jumping back to the three girls, who were talking intently as they reached the barn. Suddenly, Haze lifted her head and looked in the direction of the woods, her ears twitching. Amara felt a shiver of unease run down her spine.

They waited until the coast was clear then ran through the gently falling flakes of snow to the closest horsebox. They hid behind it, checked again and then ran to the next one and the next until they were at the gap in the fence. Then they sprinted, hearts pounding and breath coming in gasps as they ran up the steep path that led into the tree clearing where Kalini was waiting. The ponies whinnied as they saw their riders and came to meet them. White flakes were melting in Ember's black mane as he nuzzled Amara's cold face.

"Did you find anything out?" Kalini asked.

Amara nodded. "Loads!" She took hold of

Ember's reins and put her foot in the stirrup to mount.

Alex had already vaulted on to Rose, not bothering with his stirrups. "They *have* been sabotaging us and the other teams, and they're using some kind of magic reins that give them control of their ponies' powers, and they're going to use them in the competition!"

Kalini looked shocked. "What kind of reins?"

"Daniela called them binding reins," said Amara. "I bet they're made using the same kind of magic Ivy made that binding halter with when she tried to capture Ember." She remembered what they'd overheard Zara saying. "And we heard Zara say she's had an idea, something else to try and stop us."

"We've got to tell Jill!" Imogen said, gathering up her reins. "Come on!"

Before they could move, there was a rustle in the trees and Scorch, Haze and Quake burst on to the path. Their riders, Zara, Shannon and Daniela, sneered, brandishing their riding crops!

CHAPTER EIGHT

"Haze was right. She said she heard horses out here," said Shannon.

"What are you lot doing?" Daniela demanded.

"If you've come to try and spy on us, you can think again!" said Zara, her eyes narrowing.

Amara realised that the Night Riders thought they'd only just arrived – they didn't know that they had seen them practising.

"You're the ones who need to think again!" Alex said angrily. "If you believe you can get away with . . ."

"Threatening us!" Amara shouted, drowning out Alex. The last thing she wanted Alex to do was let Zara and the other two know they'd found out about the binding reins. "You can forget it," she went on. "It's not going to work."

Alex gave her a confused look, but Imogen also seemed to have picked up on how little the Night Riders knew. "This is a public bridleway," she said quickly. "You can't stop us riding here."

"That's what you think!" snapped Zara. She nodded at Daniela and Quake stamped one of his front hooves on the ground hard.

A ripple ran through the earth, heading

like a snake towards the Moonlight Stables riders and their horses.

The horses whinnied in alarm as the ground under their hooves shook.

Zara hooted with laughter. "Changed your mind about leaving yet? If not, maybe this will convince you!"

Scorch stamped her hooves and a fireball erupted from the ground. Amara gasped. Scorch was a fire horse like Ember but she wasn't as powerful, and Amara had never seen her create a fireball before. It shot towards them like a bowling ball made of flames.

Ember banged his hooves down, sending a fireball of his own to meet it. The two fireballs collided, sending sparks and flames shooting up into the sky, heating the air up and turning the falling snow to rain.

"Ready to show them what we think of spies?" cried Zara.

"Ready!" the other two shouted back, and they kicked their horses on, charging straight at Amara and the others, their crops in the air. Even though they were still in their ordinary shape, the Storm Stables ponies' speed was incredible. They flew towards Ember, Thunder, Rose and Tide. The Moonlight Stables ponies swung round to gallop away but they were too slow. The Storm Stables ponies were almost on top of them, their riders lashing out gleefully with the crops. Then suddenly the Storm Stables ponies started to slip and slide. Amara realised that the ground under their hooves was now covered with a thick layer of ice.

She had no idea where it had come from, but she saw their chance. As Zara, Daniela and Shannon struggled to stay on their ponies, Amara shrieked at her friends and their horses.

"Let's go!"

No one needed telling twice. The horses transformed into their elemental forms and were soon racing away up the hill and on to the ridgeway. They galloped faster than they had ever gone before, speeding through the

falling snow, across the open ground and then finally into the trees and back down the hill to Moonlight Stables, only changing back into ponies when they reached the end of the woods and emerged on to the lane.

Amara's thoughts raced. *What just happened? How did we get away?*

"Where did that ice come from?" demanded Alex. "Which of your horses made it?"

"It definitely wasn't Ember," said Amara.

"Or Tide," said Imogen.

"I don't think it was any of us," said Kalini. "It just appeared."

"Well, I'm very glad it did," said Amara shakily. "Their ponies were so fast."

"How could they be that quick when they weren't in their elemental shape?" said Alex.

"I don't know," said Imogen. "But we need to talk to Jill right now!"

As soon as the ponies were settled, Jill made them all mugs of hot chocolate in the tack room and listened to everything that had happened.

"We don't know where the ice on the ground came from," said Imogen. "None of the horses can make ice. Could it have been one of the Storm Stables horses' magic that went wrong?"

Jill shook her head. "I think you were just lucky. The fireballs exploding together would have heated up the air and turned the snow that was falling to rain. When the rain hit the frozen ground, the sudden drop in temperature would have turned the water drops back into ice, causing an ice sheet to form wherever they touched. It's a natural weather phenomenon called freezing rain."

"Well, I'm very glad it happened," said Amara. The others nodded.

"What are we going to do about those binding reins that Storm Stables are using?" said Kalini.

Jill rubbed her forehead, the furrows deepening. "I hoped I'd never see a binding rein again. When they are attached to both sides of the metal bit in a horse's mouth, they increase the power a horse has and put that power under the control of the rider. Not only is it really wrong for a human to use an elemental horse's power against their will, but it's also dangerous. The magic is very strong and it can be hard to control. Last time Ivy used a binding rein – well . . ." Jill's face became a mask of pain. "It caused the death of my horse, Shula."

They all stared, shocked. Jill almost never mentioned Shula.

Amara broke the silence. "What . . . what happened?"

Jill took a breath. "Ivy and I became True Riders within a few months of each other. Shula was a very powerful fire horse and Ivy had Bolt, an air horse who could create lightning. At first it was good to have someone to share the magic with, but Ivy was always very competitive and she didn't like that Shula's powers were greater than Bolt's. It drove a wedge between us and we fell out. As well as being True Riders, we also both competed in show jumping classes. Bolt and Shula were both very talented and we were often competing for the top two places. When we were sixteen, we both qualified for the finals of a big, national competition. Around that time, Ivy discovered binding ropes and learnt how they could be turned into reins, which would increase an elemental horse's power and put it under the complete control of the rider. She wanted Bolt to have her elemental speed and strength in the competition to give her the best chance of winning, and so she made binding reins. But a few days before the competition, Ivy lost control of the power and lightning started striking all around her. I was riding past on Shula and saw what was happening. I got off Shula and ran over. All I was thinking was that if I could unclip the reins, the power would escape back into nature and they would both be safe, but as I was unclipping them, lightning forked down at me." Jill swallowed. "Shula knocked me out of the way just in time, taking the full force of the lightning herself. She died instantly."

They all drew in their breath, imagining the horror of what it would be like to lose their horses.

"I crouched beside my beautiful, loyal Shula, and Ivy . . . Ivy just screamed at me and told me it was my own fault for interfering. There were fires all around us where the lightning had struck trees and bushes. I threw the reins on to one of them and they burnt to cinders. I thought – I hoped – I would never see binding reins ever again." Jill swallowed and rubbed a hand over her eyes.

Amara didn't know what to say. It was awful, but at least now she understood why there was so much bad feeling between Jill and Ivy.

"We need to get those binding reins the Storm Stables lot are using," said Alex.

Jill nodded. "This is about much more than just winning the competition; they could put themselves in serious danger using binding reins. But it's not going to be easy to get them and destroy them. The horses' powers will be heightened."

"Which is why Quake is suddenly able to cause the ground to rip apart so violently from such a distance, and Haze is able to cause fog that's so thick and lasts such a long time," said Imogen.

"And why Scorch can make fireballs now," said Amara.

Jill nodded.

Zara's words from earlier echoed in Amara's head: *I've got an idea . . .* She felt a prickle creep down her spine. What exactly was Zara planning?

"If only there was a way we could increase our horses' powers," Kalini said.

"Well, actually, there is," said Jill thoughtfully. "Your horses can learn to boost each other's magic, which can be useful if you're under attack. It's difficult to do and relies on you trusting and understanding each other, but I think you four are ready to master it. I can teach you if you'd like?"

"Yes!" they all declared.

"Then ask your parents to drop you off early tomorrow and meet me in the meadow at 8 a.m.," Jill replied. "I'll show you what to do and then we can try to get those binding reins and destroy them."

Amara felt hope rise inside her. Maybe there was a way they could stop Zara, Daniela and Shannon after all!

CHAPTER NINE

Amara had so many thoughts tumbling round in her head, she didn't sleep well that night. Early in the morning she checked her phone. It was still dark outside but she decided to go and see Ember.

She could tell from the frost on her bedroom windows that it was another cold day. She bundled up with lots of layers and two pairs of thick socks before eating a piece of toast and leaving a note for her parents.

She pulled a fluorescent yellow hat with a built-in head torch over her plaits, put on her wellies, gloves and coat and set off.

She was right about the cold – the freezing air cut like a knife and her breath puffed out in white clouds. It hadn't snowed, but the light of her head torch showed her that all the bare branches of the trees and every blade of grass were covered with a thick layer of white frost. As she turned on to the lane, she stepped on a frozen puddle and almost fell over. Taking more care, she skirted around the patches of ice, using the headtorch to light her way. The lane was so slippery, she moved to the edge of it so she could walk on the narrow grass verge where the ice was less dangerous. *There's no way we can bring the ponies out on to this*, she thought. *They could easily fall. We'll have to stick to the school until the ice melts.*

The frozen grass crunched under her feet as she made her way along the lane. The sun was rising now, streaking the black sky with bursts of grey, and a bitter wind was blowing in occasional gusts that made her catch her breath. As she got near to the entrance to the stables, she heard a whinny from the meadow. *Was that Ember?* She quickened her pace. Jill must have turned the ponies out already.

As she reached the fence that separated the meadow from the lane, she saw Bea on the groundwork course in the dawn light, using a leadrope and long wand to guide a pony over poles and around barrels. But it wasn't Sandy; it was Forest, and he was looking tense, jumping over the poles instead of stepping over them and shying away from the sheet of tarpaulin on the ground. The other ponies were watching from near the fence. Amara was about to call out to Bea and ask what she was doing when Bea unclipped the throat strap of Forest's headcollar.

"OK, Forest. Let's try it without a headcollar." Bea's voice carried to Amara. "I bet you trust me enough now."

As she started to pull the headcollar over his ears, a gust of wind caught the edge of the tarpaulin and it flapped upwards, making a noise. Forest shied back, the headcollar catching on one ear.

He shook his head in a panic, making the headcollar flap against his face. The feel of

it seemed to panic him even more. "Forest! Whoa!" Bea cried, but Forest careered away. Shaking his head, he galloped towards the fence and then Amara saw something that made her blood freeze in her veins. The gate that led on to the lane had swung open in the breeze. Bea must have let herself into the meadow that way and not shut it properly behind her!

Amara's hands flew to her mouth. If Forest got out on to the lane, he was bound to slip and fall. She started to run along the grass verge, but she could already tell there was no way she would reach it before the frightened pony.

Suddenly, she saw Sandy charging along the side of the fence. She reached the gateway just before Forest did and blocked it off. Forest tried to stop but his hooves slipped on the frosty grass. He started to slide back.

Amara gasped. He was going to fall! Then

suddenly, a carpet of golden sand appeared under his hooves. It gave him the grip he needed and instead of falling he managed to stay upright. He stopped, his head high, his eyes wide, his sides heaving.

Sandy stepped forward, her eyes gentle. She nuzzled Forest's neck. Amara saw Forest's head lower as Bea reached them. "Oh, Sandy, thank you!" she said, throwing her arms round the palomino pony's neck. "You used your magic and stopped him from hurting himself!"

Amara hurried into the field, shutting the gate behind her. "Bea, what were you doing?"

Bea burst into tears. "I wanted a chance to see if I might be Forest's True Rider. I thought if I came here first thing and worked with him on my own, he might just choose me like Ember chose you. But it all went wrong." She sniffed. "I feel so stupid. What if he'd hurt himself?"

"He didn't; that's the important thing," said Amara.

"Thanks to Sandy," said Bea, looking gratefully at the palomino pony.

Sandy snuffled at Bea's tear-stained face. Bea reluctantly laughed. "Sandy, that tickles!" Sandy did it again, her eyes filled with cheeky delight. Then she pushed her head against Bea's jacket pocket. Bea stroked her face. "You're trying to tell me you deserve a treat?"

Sandy blinked at her.

Bea grinned. "You deserve a whole packet for managing to control your magic like that," she said, getting a tube of mints from her pocket and giving Sandy three of them. "But that wouldn't be good for your teeth." Sandy nudged her hand. "OK, OK, just one more," Bea said.

Amara chuckled. "You might not be Sandy's True Rider yet, but you already seem to be able to read her mind!"

Bea ruffled Sandy's forelock and heaved a sigh. "Do you think she'll ever choose me, Amara?"

Amara remembered what Ember had said about Sandy being a patient horse who would take her time to decide rather than rushing into things. "I bet she will," she said. "You just may have to wait a bit longer."

Bea looked happier. "I'll wait, Sandy,' she whispered. "I don't mind how long it takes. You're the perfect pony for me."

Sandy lifted her muzzle and snuffled at her nose, making Bea giggle again. "So, how come you're here so early?" she asked Amara.

Amara explained that Jill was going to teach her and the others how to help their ponies boost each other's powers.

"Do you think she'll let me watch?" Bea asked.

"I'm sure she will," said Amara.

She was right. When Jill got to the meadow, she looked momentarily surprised to see Bea there with her arm around Sandy but she didn't ask any questions, and when Kalini, Alex and Imogen arrived, she let Bea observe their lesson.

First of all, Jill asked Ember, Tide, Thunder and Rose to transform. Sitting on Ember bareback, Amara could feel the flickering flames of his mane licking her fingers, warming them but not burning. Jill addressed the horses.

"Each of you knows how to conjure, use and control your powers and how to communicate with your riders," she said. "In order to strengthen another elemental horse's magic, you must collect the power inside you and then you and your rider must focus on the horse you wish to help. Your minds must be perfectly in tune, and at the exact same moment you must release the power to boost the other horse's magic. Let's have a try. Stand in a circle and take it in turns to help the horse on your left. We'll start with Ember strengthening Rose's magic."

Putting her hand on Ember's neck, Amara

felt the power building inside him as he drew it in. It felt like his skin was crackling under her fingertips and then she heard his voice.

I think I can do this, Amara. Let's count to three then pass power to Rose.

Shutting her eyes, Amara let her mind merge with Ember's as they counted down together: *One . . . two . . . THREE!*

ROSE! they both thought at the same time. Amara felt the extra power that had been building up stream from Ember to Rose. As it reached the chestnut horse, her mane and tail turned a brighter shade of green, her silver eyes sparkled even more brightly and the strands of her chestnut coat shone as if coated in gold. She stamped her hoof down and a young oak tree burst from the ground in the centre of the circle. It shot upwards, its trunk widening and expanding, its branches shooting out until Rose stamped her hoof again and the tree stopped.

"Whoa!" breathed Alex, for once looking almost lost for words. "That felt awesome. Like the normal rush of power but times a hundred. And you made a tree, Rose – an actual tree!" The Earth Horse snorted. Alex looked at the others. "She said it felt easy."

"Great work!" said Jill, beaming. "OK, this time, Alex, you and Rose boost Tide's power."

One by one the ponies and their riders practised. And then rather than working round the circle they chose someone to help simply by using eye contact. By the end of the practice session, they were all buzzing. Amara felt exhilarated. Transferring magic took a huge amount of concentration but it felt amazing.

"You've all done brilliantly," said Jill. "I need to try and think of a way we can safely get the binding reins from Storm Stables but for now, I think it's time to take a break. Let's get the horses some food and then I think you could all do with breakfast too."

While they fed the ponies, Jill cooked bacon sandwiches and brought out a huge trayful. When no one could eat a single bite more, they set to work on the stable chores – mucking out the stables, refilling water buckets and stuffing hay into haynets. They all worked cheerfully, helping each other. No one bickered, no one argued. Concentrating so hard on each other as they had helped their horses boost each other's power seemed to have forged a strong new connection between them. Even Bea, who hadn't taken part, seemed to feel it. The sensation of togetherness and being a team continued throughout their practice. They were all more aware of each other, making eye contact, trying to read each other's moves, staying calm when mistakes were made. It was the best practice they'd had for ages.

Afterwards, Bea said she wanted to do some more groundwork with Sandy and the other four headed out happily for a ride in the woods. It was still very frosty and cold and they had to make sure the ponies used the grass verge rather than walking on the icy puddles in the lane.

In the shelter of the trees, the ground was softer and they let the ponies trot and then canter along the track before slowing down as they neared the top of the hill.

"I can't believe it's the championships tomorrow," said Kalini, patting Thunder.

"That was such a good practice," said Imogen.

"We have to get hold of the Storm Stables team's binding reins before the competition so they can't cheat," said Alex.

"And stop them putting themselves in danger," said Imogen. "I don't like Zara, Daniela or Shannon but I don't want them or their horses to be hurt."

"Or worse," said Amara with a shiver as she remembered what had happened to Shula. "Ivy should never have made those binding reins."

"She's evil," agreed Kalini as they rode out on to the ridgeway. "She doesn't care about the danger she's putting the ponies and their riders in; she just wants them to win."

A familiar, mean laugh rang out behind them. "Well, luckily so do we!"

Amara swung round and saw Zara, Shannon and Daniela riding out of the trees, blocking the entrance to the bridleway. It was Zara who had spoken. Her eyes glinted menacingly. "And you're the ones who should be worried about getting hurt!"

CHAPTER TEN

Amara felt a lurch of fear as the three Storm Stables ponies suddenly transformed. Scorch's mane and tail blazed with red fire, Haze's swirled like the deepest grey fog and Quake's became as black as coal.

"Zara!" Imogen exclaimed. "You have to stop this! Has Ivy told you the danger you're in? Has she told you about what happened to Jill's horse, Shula?"

Amara saw a look of uncertainty flash

across Zara's face but a second later it was gone. "Of course," she scoffed. "She's told us everything."

Amara was sure Zara was lying. "Ivy used a binding rein on Bolt. She couldn't control the power and Shula ended up dying!"

"If you lose control, you could be in terrible danger," said Imogen.

"Enough!" A voice as sharp as an icicle cut through the air and Ivy rode Bolt out from the trees. "You know what to do!" she hissed at the three girls. "Get on with it!"

Haze stamped her hooves and a thick freezing fog surrounded the Moonlight Stables riders. It was so dense Amara couldn't even see her hands on Ember's reins.

"Transform!" she shouted to Ember as the ground began to tremble.

She felt the power surge through him and the next moment he was rearing up, his mane and tail flaming brightly. Next to her, she could sense the other horses transforming too, but the ground was shaking harder now and they all staggered, trying to keep their balance. Rose knocked into Tide, sending her to her knees.

Amara's stomach clenched with fear. Zara, Daniela and Shannon seemed determined to hurt them and their horses.

"We've got to get away from here!" cried Kalini as Thunder staggered too.

But the ground was shaking so hard the horses couldn't move. From beyond the fog they heard Ivy's harsh laugh and the delighted shouts of the three girls.

"Oh dear – it looks like the Moonlight

Stables team is going to have to withdraw because of injuries tomorrow," exclaimed Ivy.

Use your power to burn the fog away, Ember, thought Amara.

I can't see well enough. I might hit Rose, Tide or Thunder if I create a fireball, he replied desperately.

Overhead Amara heard a sudden, sharp crackle of electricity. Looking up, she saw a flash of intense white light in the sky, a round ball of lightning that illuminated the grey clouds. Fingers of bright white light reached out across the sky like glowing cracks. Fear shot through her. It was Bolt using her power! What did Ivy have planned?

Alex yelled to the others. "Boost Rose's power NOW!"

Amara didn't stop to ask why. *Ember,*

quick! She felt the power surge through him.

One . . . two . . . THREE!

They both sent the power on to Rose just as the light above them seemed to grow brighter right in the centre of the ball.

"NOW!" hissed Ivy through the fog.

A fork of lightning shot down, heading straight towards the ground and them . . .

But at the same time as Ivy had spoken, Rose had stamped her hooves and a sapling tree had shot up from the ground between them and the Storm Stables horses. The lightning changed course, forking away from the Moonlight Stables riders, attracted to the tall, slender tree. It hit the top of it.

With a loud bang, the tree exploded into a mass of fiery shards and flames. The heat of the explosion burned away the fog around it. Amara could see the shock on Zara, Shannon and Daniela's faces and the fury on Ivy's as their horses leapt back to avoid the burning fragments. Haze and Quake lost concentration in their panic; the ground stopped shaking and the fog faded.

"Keep giving Rose power!" yelled Alex.

Amara and Ember redoubled their efforts and suddenly creepers sprang from the ground, coiling around the Storm Stables horses' hooves and twining up their legs. The horses fought against the creepers but only Bolt broke free. Amara saw her about to rear and stamp her hooves again.

"Ember!" she gasped, but before Ember could react, a tornado shot from Thunder and swept straight at Bolt, knocking her over on to her side and sending Ivy sprawling on to the ground. Creepers instantly twisted up around Ivy's wrists and ankles, holding her fast.

"Get the binding reins while Rose and I hold them with her magic!" Alex shouted.

Amara scrambled down from Ember's back and sprinted towards the struggling Storm Stables horses, whose legs were now enveloped in ivy. Kalini and Imogen followed. Throwing herself at Scorch, Amara reached for the clips that held the binding reins to her bit, just as Kalini and Imogen did the same with Haze and Quake.

"No," Zara screeched, leaning down from Scorch's back and swinging her crop towards Amara.

Amara ducked. The crop grazed her shoulder but her coat was thick and it

absorbed the blow. Amara undid the clips
and yanked the reins out of Zara's hands,
flinging them away towards Ember. Scorch
immediately whinnied in delight.

"Rose, let Scorch go!" cried Amara.

The creepers sank back into the ground
and Scorch was free! The chestnut horse,
furious at having had her power controlled,
reared up. With no reins to hold on to, Zara
flung her arms round Scorch's neck but

Scorch had had enough. She didn't try to help her rider stay on. Flinging her head down between her knees, she bucked hard – kicking her hind legs high into the air and twisting her body. Zara didn't have a chance. She flew off.

Around them, the same thing was happening with Haze and Quake. Free from the control of the hated reins, they bucked Shannon and Daniela off and turned and galloped down the hill. Bolt took one last look at Ivy and followed them. It seemed that none of the horses – even the Storm Stables horses – approved of their riders using the reins.

Amara raced back to Ember and vaulted back on as Zara, Shannon and Daniela scrambled to their feet.

"Give us the reins back!" said Zara through gritted teeth.

"No!" cried Amara. She urged Ember forward so that he was standing in front of the three pairs of blue reins coiled on the ground near the trees. "You're not having them."

"Oh, really?" Zara said, striding forward.

"Stay back!" shouted Amara, wondering in the back of her mind where Imogen and Kalini were and why they weren't helping. "Or else!"

"Or else what?" Zara sneered. "You and Ember won't do anything, Amara. You haven't got the killer instinct."

Amara put a hand out to grab her but Zara dodged out of her reach and ran towards the reins – but then she stopped abruptly, her mouth falling open. Amara stared too, a sharp shock running through her as a pure white elemental horse stepped out of the trees and stood guard over the reins!

CHAPTER ELEVEN

The mare's mane and tail were made of snowflakes. She was snow white with small flurries swirling around her hooves. She scraped one foot on the floor like an angry bull. Zara took an uncertain step backwards. "Whose horse is that?"

"Be careful, Zara," called Daniela, her voice high with fear. "It looks angry."

Amara had been feeling as shocked as the Storm Stables riders when she saw the

snow mare, but looking round wildly for her friends she suddenly saw that Thunder and Tide were standing close together, staring at the mare and concentrating hard. Kalini and Imogen were stroking their horses' necks and whispering to them.

It's not real, Amara realised with a shock. *Thunder and Tide are uniting their powers* like when they made the Christmas tree. Tide's pulled water into the air and Thunder is freezing it into snow and shaping it to look like a horse.

The snow mare trembled slightly. Amara had a sudden vision of the Christmas tree they'd made exploding.

Ember! Thunder and Tide need help. Can we boost their power?

I'll try!

Amara felt Ember gather power inside him and then they sent it racing through the air to Tide and Thunder. Their eyes widened as the power hit them and then suddenly the snow mare grew. She reared up, her front legs striking out. Zara yelped, then turned and started to run. The snow mare landed and charged at her. The three girls shrieked in fear and turned and ran down the hill, slipping and sliding on the icy ground as they tried to escape the snow mare. The mare reared up again at the top of the path and then dissolved into snowflakes.

"Come back, you cowards!" screeched Ivy. "It's just a trick!" But Zara, Daniela and Shannon were too far away to hear. Rose let the plants loosen their grip on Ivy and they disappeared back into the ground. Ivy got to her feet, her immaculate clothes and glossy boots smudged with dirt, her hair dishevelled. She stepped towards the reins, her face furious, but suddenly all four Moonlight Stables horses were there, standing side by side.

"Go!" said Imogen coldly.

Ivy looked like she was going to argue, but

without Bolt she had no power.

Ember stamped and conjured a fireball. He started rolling it slowly towards Ivy, who backed away. "You'll be sorry for this!" she hissed, and then she turned and ran off down the path. Ember stamped his hoof and the fireball exploded at the top of the path.

"Oh dear – it's a long way home," said Imogen with a grin. "And those posh riding boots she wears really don't look very comfy."

"We've got the binding reins," said Kalini, her voice shaky with relief as she turned to look at the heap of blue rope. "What should we do with them?"

"Burn them," said Amara. She jumped off Ember, grabbed the reins and ran to the fire Ember had made. "Agreed?" she said to the others as she held the reins over the flames.

"Agreed!" they cried. Amara threw the reins on to the fire. The flames turned blue and sparks shot up into the sky. Amara and the others watched until the flames died down and all that was left was a pile of blue ash.

With a stamp of his hoof, Thunder conjured a gust of wind that caught the ash and spiralled it up into the air, whisking it away and scattering it across the ridgeway. The binding reins had finally been destroyed!

Jill was astonished when they got back and told her what had happened. "This is incredible," she said. "It sounds like you were very quick-thinking and used your horses' powers brilliantly. I couldn't ask for a better team of True Riders."

"Or a better mounted games team," said Alex with a grin. "Now that Storm Stables can't cheat, we might actually beat them tomorrow."

"Whatever happens in the final, I couldn't be prouder of you," said Jill, pulling them into a group hug. "Win or lose, it doesn't matter. The important thing is that you have stopped Zara, Daniela and Shannon and their horses from potentially getting hurt."

Imogen chuckled. "I don't think they'll be saying thank you any time soon."

"No, but you know you helped your horses to do good and that's all that matters," said Jill. "Now, I think you all need some lunch and then it's time to get the horses and tack cleaned up for the competition.

Malia's coming to help, and Jasmine and Ollie. Afterwards, hot chocolate and cakes at Marco's – my treat. Does that sound like a good plan?"

"Definitely!" they all chorused.

It was great fun getting the horses ready. Knowing the binding reins had been destroyed was a huge weight off their shoulders and they worked happily, filling buckets with warm water, rubbing shampoo into the ponies' coats and rinsing them clean. They couldn't use magic because their friend Malia was helping, but when she was busy fetching hoof oil from the tack room, Sirocco conjured up a blast of warm air to help the other ponies' coats dry.

"Wow," said Malia when she got back and stopped to stroke Ember. "He's dried really quickly."

"Yeah," said Amara, hiding her grin. "They all have." She saw a puzzled, slightly suspicious look cross Malia's face as she glanced down the row of perfectly dry ponies. She remembered feeling like that herself about the strange things that seemed to happen on the yard before she had found out about the elemental magic.

"Are you still going to be able to come and help out at the competition tomorrow?" she asked Malia as a distraction.

"Yep; I'm the equipment girl," said Malia cheerfully. Every team had to nominate someone who could help move the equipment between races.

"Do you think you'd ever like to do mounted games?" Amara asked her curiously as Malia went to pat Forest, who was looking out of his stable.

Malia stroked Forest's face and he rested his chin on her shoulder. "I would. It always looks like loads of fun when you lot are practising. But I wouldn't really be able to compete in a team because of all the dressage I do, and I definitely wouldn't be allowed to do it on Goldie in case she hurt herself."

"Maybe you should ask Jill if you can join in some training sessions with Forest after Christmas," said Amara. "She's not sure he'll ever make a competitive games pony, but it would do him good to train and be ridden regularly."

Malia nodded thoughtfully. "Maybe."

Amara felt a stab of hope. It would be amazing if Malia could become Forest's True Rider and Bea could become Sandy's.

She turned back happily to Ember. After a dramatic start to the day and the danger they had been in on the hillside, it was beginning to feel as if everything might work out after all!

CHAPTER TWELVE

"You can do it, Amara!"

"Go, Ember!"

"Come on, Moonlight Stables!"

As she waited on the start line for the first race – the bending race – Amara's heart pounded with excitement at the encouragement from her teammates. Zara was lined up next to her, her face determined. Beyond her were the riders from Hillside Farm and Long Lane.

The umpire's flag fell and they were off!

Ember raced up the line of poles, weaving in and out of them, then turned incredibly sharply at the top, neck and neck with Scorch. On the way back, Amara urged him on even faster and he pulled away from Scorch.

"Go on, you stupid horse," yelled Zara, her heels drumming against Scorch's sides. Scorch's ears flattened and instead of going faster she slowed down. It appeared she hadn't forgiven Zara for the binding reins quite yet.

Ember raced across the line first, Amara handing the baton perfectly to Kalini. As she pulled Ember up, Amara came face to face with Zara, who was scowling. "What's up, Zara? Don't you have the killer instinct today?" Amara called, grinning at the furious expression on Zara's face as she trotted to join the rest of her teammates.

The Storm Stables team were soon out of the running for the cup. Although the boys' ponies were as fast as ever, Haze, Scorch and Quake seemed to be going out of their way to hinder their riders. They stopped that little bit too far away from the buckets in the sock race so that their riders missed when they tried to throw the rolled-up socks inside. They shied just as their riders tried to place a plastic carton on top of a pile of other plastic cartons, and swerved slightly to one side in the mug race so the riders missed the mugs when they tried to grab them.

In contrast, the Moonlight Stables ponies did everything they could to help their riders and Amara felt a new connection between her and the rest of her team, a connection that had come both from their practice and from learning how to use magic together. She found she could read Alexs, Imogens and Kalini's body language better than ever before and when they made eye contact, it was almost as though they could read each other's minds. She had never felt so in tune with them. Their handovers were great, they encouraged each other and even when the occasional mistake was made, no one got cross or upset. It was just the best feeling.

The other teams were really good too though. Hillside Farm managed brilliantly with just four riders and Long Lane had clearly been working hard to help the black-and-white pony on their team get over its fear of barrels.

In the final race – the flag race – Long Lane just managed to beat the others over the finish line and were announced as the overall winners. Moonlight Stables and Long Lane were joint runners up and Storm Stables came a long way behind in fourth place.

The Moonlight Stables and Hillside Farm riders clapped as Long Lane were given the champions' cup. Ivy stormed away and the Storm Stables team watched sulkily, refusing to clap as Long Lane did a lap of honour.

"Well done!" Amara and the other team members called to each other as they all left the arena.

"We'll beat you next year though!" Alex shouted with a grin to the Long Lane team.

"In your dreams!" they shouted back.

Amara and the others rode off round the ground, rosettes fluttering from both sides of their ponies' bridles.

"That was such a fun competition," said Kalini.

"The ponies were amazing," said Imogen, hugging Tide.

"Just one point in it," said Alex. "We so could have won."

"We have won, really, though," said Amara.

"How?" said Kalini.

Amara smiled. "We win because we get to take home the best ponies." She stroked Ember's silky neck as the others – even Alex – nodded in agreement.

"We also win because we're the best team of True Riders and we just defeated Ivy Thornton!" said Imogen happily.

"Hey, it's snowing!" said Kalini suddenly,

pointing upwards. Flakes had started to drift down from the sky.

Thunder checked around then swirled up a wind to make the flakes come together in the shape of a little snow horse.

Amara held her hand up. "Moonlight Stables for ever!"

Her friends' hands met hers in a high five. "Moonlight Stables for ever!" they all cried as the tiny snow mare reared triumphantly in the air.

The End

True Rider: Amara Thompson

Age:
10

Appearance:
Brown hair and blue eyes

Lives with:
Parents

Best friend:
Kalini

Favourite things to do:
Anything with horses, drawing and reading pony stories

Favourite mounted game:
Bending race

I most want to improve:
Vaulting on and off at speed and getting my handovers right

Elemental Horse: Ember

Colour:
Black

Height:
14.1hh

Personality:
Loving, lively, hot-tempered

Pony breed:
Welsh section B x
Thoroughbred

Elemental appearance:
Golden eyes, swirling mane and a magical, fiery tail

Elemental abilities:
Fire Horse - Ember can create fires, make things burst into flame and cast fireballs from his hooves

True Rider: Imogen Fairfax

Age:
10

Appearance:
Light brown hair and hazel eyes

Lives with:
Mum, Dad, two brothers Will (17)
and Tim (15), Minnie our cockapoo

Best friend:
Alex

Favourite things to do:
Anything with horses, walking
Minnie, helping at my gran's
teashop

Favourite mounted game:
Mug shuffle

I most want to improve:
My accuracy in races

Elemental Horse: Tide

Colour:
White-grey

Height:
14.1hh

Personality:
Thoughtful, sensitive and kind

Pony breed:
Arab x Welsh

Elemental appearance:
Blue eyes, silver-blue coat and a
flowing sea foam mane and tail

Elemental abilities:
Water Horse - Tide can make
it rain and manipulate bodies
of water to create waves,
whirlpools and waterspouts

True Rider: Alex Brahler

Age:
11

Appearance:
Black hair and dark brown eyes

Lives with:
Mum, Dad, sister Frankie
(15) and our chocolate Labradors,
Scooby and Murphy

Best friend:
Imogen

Favourite things to do:
Anything with horses, playing
football, cross-country running,
climbing and swimming

Favourite mounted game:
Five-flag race

I most want to improve:
Being more patient in
competitions so I'm not
eliminated by starting races
before the flag falls!

Elemental Horse: Rose

Colour:
Bright chestnut with flaxen
mane and tail, a white blaze
and four white socks

Height:
14.2 hh

Personality:
Patient, calm, confident

Pony Breed:
Welsh section C

Elemental appearance:
Bright green eyes, a mossy green
mane and tail covered in flowers

Elemental abilities:
Earth Horse - Rose can make plants
and flowers grow

Night Rider: Zara Watson

Age:
11

Appearance:
Blonde hair and green eyes

Lives with:
Mum most of the time
and Dad some of the time

Best friend:
Daniela (my cousin)

Favourite things to do:
Riding, playing tennis, shopping,
pamper sessions

Favourite mounted game:
Bottle race

I most want to improve:
Nothing, I'm good at everything

Elemental Horse: Scorch

Colour:
Bright chestnut with a white blaze

Height:
14.2hh

Personality:
Lively, mean, impatient

Pony Breed:
Show Pony x Thoroughbred

Elemental appearance:
Red eyes, mane and tail of dark
flickering flames

Elemental abilities:
Fire Horse - although not as
powerful as Ember, Scorch can heat
things up and cause small fires

Moonlight Riders

Meet all the True Riders of Moonlight
Stables and their amazing elemental horses!

Fire Horse
LINDA CHAPMAN

Storm Stallion
LINDA CHAPMAN

Petal Pony
LINDA CHAPMAN

Sea Foal
LINDA CHAPMAN

Snow Mare
LINDA CHAPMAN

Sand Filly
LINDA CHAPMAN

Do you have what it takes to become a True Rider?